NORTHFIELD BRANCH
(847) 446-5990

S0-BZU-963

JANUARY
2022

**Winnetka-Northfield Public
Library District
Winnetka, IL 60093**
(847) 446-7220

The Treasure Box

written by **DAVE KEANE**

illustrated by **RAHELE JOMEPOUR BELL**

putnam

G. P. PUTNAM'S SONS

For Pa & Grandma and Big Grandpa & Grammy –D.K.

For Madarjaan and Grandma Gloria, Grandma Jean, Grandma Kay, Grandma Feri, Grandma Suzanne, and Grandpa Dan –R.J.B.

G. P. PUTNAM'S SONS
An imprint of Penguin Random House LLC, New York

Text copyright © 2022 by David J. Keane
Illustrations copyright © 2022 by Rahele Jomepour Bell
Penguin supports copyright. Copyright fuels creativity, encourages diverse voices, promotes free speech, and creates a vibrant culture. Thank you for buying an authorized edition of this book and for complying with copyright laws by not reproducing, scanning, or distributing any part of it in any form without permission. You are supporting writers and allowing Penguin to continue to publish books for every reader.

G. P. Putnam's Sons is a registered trademark of Penguin Random House LLC.

Visit us online at penguinrandomhouse.com

Library of Congress Cataloging-in-Publication Data is available.

Printed in the United States of America
ISBN 9781984813183
10   9   8   7   6   5   4   3   2   1
PC

Design by Suki Boynton ◊ Text set in Usherwood
The art was done with scanned handmade textures and collaged digitally.

I am always on the lookout.
  I look for special things to put in
my secret treasure box.

Since the last time Grandpa visited, I have found many interesting and amazing things.

A very round and very smooth rock.

A green parachute guy who lost his parachute.

A suit of dried-up skin a snake left behind.

A tiny bird's nest that has blue yarn in it.

A giant feather.

And a very,

　　very,

　　very,

　　very

　　straight stick.

That's why I'm waiting by the window.
I know he'll like to see what I found.
My collection of treasures is our secret.

When Grandpa and Grammy arrive, I have to wait for them to drink their tea and talk forever with Mommy and Daddy.

Later, Grandpa and I sneak away. He takes
a long time to get up the stairs. "I am slow,
but graceful like a cat," he says.

Grandpa always takes out his magnifying glass before I open the latch.

I make him hold the snake skin,
even though he doesn't want to.
He makes the funniest faces.

Grandpa taps his watch
and says it's time.

We go for a walk to see if
we can find any treasures.

We collect things in his little blue hat. Grandpa finds
a rusty spring and a doll's lost arm. I find a dirty marble
and a cracked-open robin's egg.

"These are perfect," I say.

When Grandpa gets sick and can't visit, I spend time
in my room looking at our collection. It reminds me
of all his funny faces.

I keep asking to go to Grandpa and Grammy's house,
and one day we finally do. Grandpa has tubes in his
nose, but he can still make funny faces.

When nobody is around, I show him two new things
I found for the treasure box. He likes them so much,
he cries a little bit.

The next time I see Grandpa, he's in a hospital.
His room has a wide-open door, beeping machines,
and a sit-up bed, but he's sound asleep anyway.

"He just needs to rest, honey," Mom says.

Before we go, I leave a few treasures. He'll know
who brought them.

One day, Mommy and Daddy come to
my room and tell me that Grandpa died.
I don't say anything.

I look out the window and pretend I
can see him waving at me.

I go with Mommy and Daddy to Grandpa's memorial,
which is a sad party you have when someone dies.
The grown-ups talk and talk and talk and talk.
    I just can't eat any of the tiny sandwiches.
    Instead, I stare at all the photos of Grandpa when he had
lots of hair and smooth skin. I say goodbye to Grandpa in my heart.

When we come home, I pull out my secret treasure box, but I don't undo the latch. I am too sad, and opening it would make it worse.

It's a long time before Grammy
comes back to visit. I watch
her out the window, and
she waves. She is all
alone now.

I listen as she drinks
tea with Mommy
and Daddy.

Then Grammy comes to my room.
"Your grandpa gave me some things
to give to you," she tells me quietly.
She pulls out Grandpa's little blue hat,
his magnifying glass, and his watch.

"He told me you would know
what to do with them," she says.
I nod.

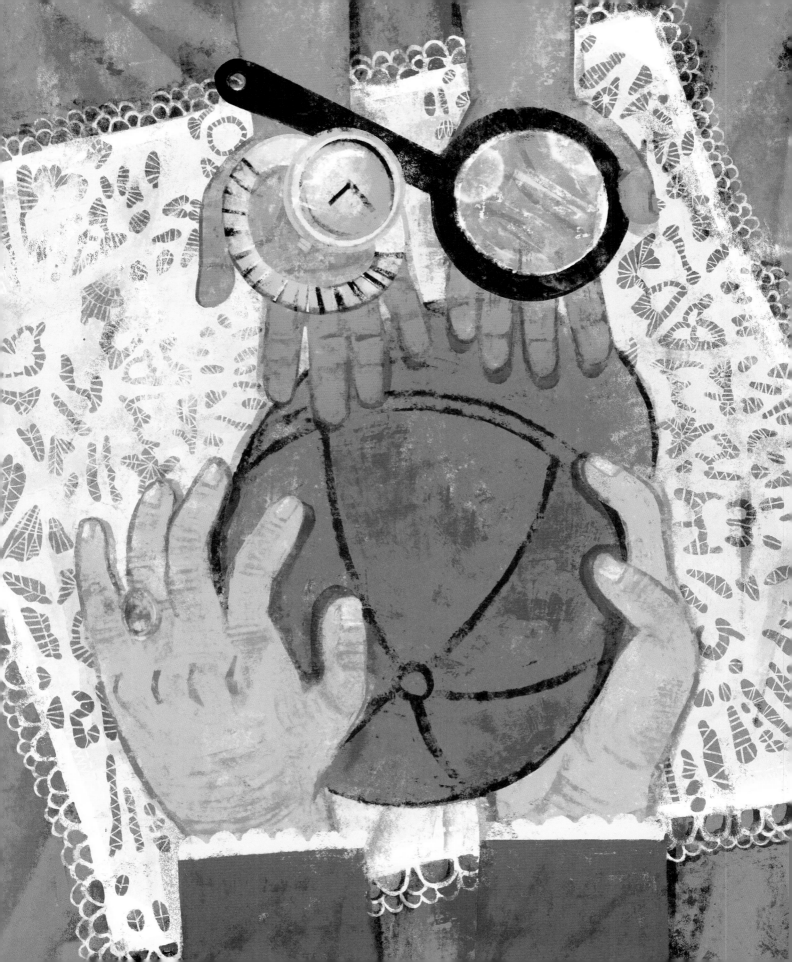

I pull out my secret treasure box and open it for
the first time since I saw Grandpa at the hospital.
"This was our secret collection of little treasures,"
I tell Grammy.

I show her the rusty spring and the doll's arm
from Grandpa's last visit. Plus some of Grandpa's
favorites. I even show her the snake skin, which
Grammy doesn't mind holding.

"So crinkly," she says.

I sit in Grammy's lap.
"I miss his funny faces,"
I finally say.
"I do too," Grammy says.

We sit and cry and think about Grandpa for a long time.
I put the magnifying glass and watch in the treasure box,
but not the little blue cap.

We use it when we go for a walk to find interesting and amazing new things for our secret treasure box.